For all those who stay true
in an ever-changing world ~ O. H.

For Finnley and Jocelyn, may your worlds be full of adventures,
but also include moments of relative calm to enjoy a nice cup of tea and a cookie ~ S. J.

tiger tales
5 River Road, Suite 128,
Wilton, CT 06897
Published in the United States 2017
Originally published in Great Britain 2017
by Little Tiger Press
Text by Owen Hart
Text copyright © 2017 Little Tiger Press
Illustrations copyright © 2017 Sean Julian
ISBN-13: 978-1-68010-070-9
ISBN-10: 1-68010-070-X
Printed in China
LTP/1800/2117/1117

For more insight and activities,
visit us at www.tigertalesbooks.com

I'll Love You Forever

by Owen Hart

Illustrated by Sean Julian

tiger tales

I'll love you forever.
I'll always be near
To share in the laughter
of each passing year.

Though seasons may turn,
bringing sights new and strange,
My love is the one thing
that won't ever change.

On crisp winter days
over icebergs we'll go.
We'll tumble and leap
through the fluffy white snow.

Come look at this snowflake
and I will explain:
In spring it will melt,
but my love will remain.

As the days become warmer,
we'll fill them with fun—
A splash in the sea,
then a snooze in the sun.

At the end of each day,
I will kiss you good night.
I never grow tired
of holding you tight.

And when the birds tell us
that summer has come,
We'll play in the grass
while the bees gently hum.

The leaves will turn golden
as fall comes along.
The flowers may fade,
but my love will stay strong.

When cold winter winds
blow the leaves far and wide,
You'll cross the great icebergs
with me by your side.

We'll both gaze in wonder
when the new buds peek through.
As each flower blossoms,
I'll share it with you.

But for now, cuddle close
while the stars softly shine.

I'll always be yours,
and you'll always be mine.

Through the change of the seasons
and each passing year,
I'll love you forever
and ever, my dear.

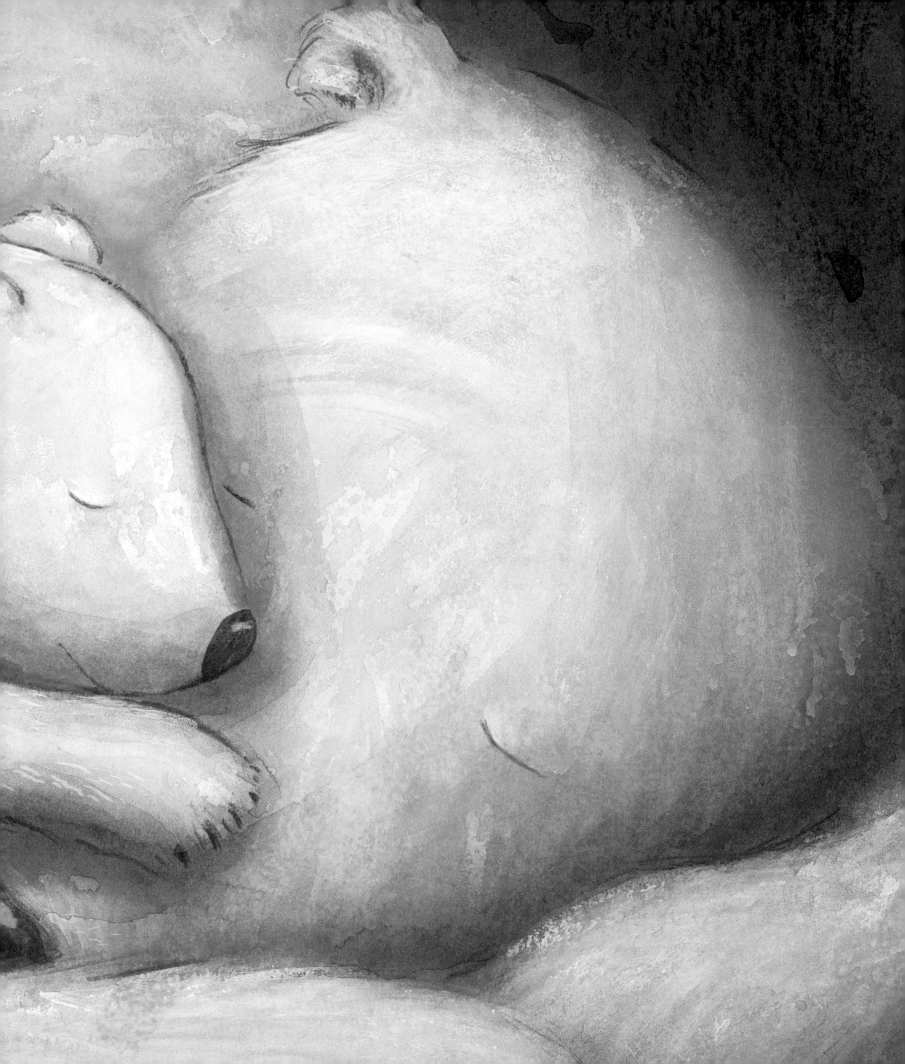